Once Upon

Adapted by Elizabeth Isele
Based upon characters created by
Rae Lambert and a screenplay written
by Mark Young and Kelly Ward

Illustrated by Carol H. Grosvenor

Turner Publishing, Inc.
ATLANTA

A FOREST

NOT SO VERY LONG AGO, a small group of Furlings lived a happy life in Dapplewood Forest. "Furling" was what a wise, old badger named Cornelius called the small, furry animals in Dapplewood. Being the oldest and wisest animal, Cornelius could teach the Furlings about everything in the forest—about things that had happened and about things that might happen. He taught the Furlings about all the good things and warned them about some dangerous and fearsome things.

One of his Furlings was a pretty young woodmouse named Abigail. Abigail was very brave for such a small creature. She loved to sit high up in an old, old tree and look out over Dapplewood Forest.

There she could hear her Furling friend, Russell the Hedgehog, struggling to get some breakfast before his 13 brothers and sisters ate everything.

Looking through the tree branches, Abigail could see another Furling, Edgar the Mole, squirm away from his mother. "Mama," he said, "Cornelius promised us a big surprise, and you are making me late for class!"

"What? No goodbye kiss?" said Mama.

"No time," said Edgar.

Abigail scooted down the tree to the ground where her father was looking for her. "See you later, Dad," she said. "I love you."

"Hurry, or we'll be late for class," Abigail called to Russell and Edgar. "I hear Michelle ringing Cornelius's bell."

Michelle was the smallest one of these four Furlings, but she was somewhat special because she was Cornelius's niece.

"Michelle, stop your ringing! We are here," panted Abigail as the Furlings skidded to a stop just inside Cornelius's door.

"Guess what? You'll never guess, so I'll tell you," said Michelle. "Uncle Cornelius said I could go with you on your nature hike today. I hope he won't forget his promise because you're late."

Abigail looked about and said, "I can hardly see him behind his papers; he must be experimenting."

"DON'T TAKE ANOTHER STEP!" shouted Cornelius from behind his desk. "Stop and prepare to be amazed!"

Suddenly a tiny birdlike plane flew out over Cornelius's piles of papers and maps and soared around his stacks of books.

"Wow, look at that! It's really flying!" said Russell.

"What do you think of my Flapper Wingamathing?" asked Cornelius. "Of course, this is just a test model. One day I shall build it full size."

"Good. Maybe he won't notice we're late," said Edgar.

"I bet he's working on the big surprise," said Michelle.

"Oh, I love surprises," said Russell. "Let's take a look."

"Can I fly it?" asked Russell.

"Don't be silly. You'll crash it," said Abigail as she dashed after the speeding Wingamathing.

"Almost had it," said Russell as he leaped across the room.

"Furlings, please be careful!" yelled Cornelius.

Edgar jumped up, knocking over a tall pile of books, and yelled, "I got it!"

But not for long. Edgar tripped over Russell and dropped the Wingamathing to the floor. A big book crashed on top of it.

"Great Honk!" said Cornelius.

Russell said, "Oh, Oh! I guess we wrecked the big surprise."

"No," said Cornelius. "The big surprise is not something I made but something I found. So let's step lively, Furlings. We can clean up this disaster later."

Later, outside, Cornelius picked a flower and put it in Michelle's hair.

Michelle hugged him and said, "Thanks for letting me come, too."

Cornelius told the Furlings, "Today is plant day, and we shall learn how everything we need—our food and even our medicine—grows right here in Dapplewood Forest."

He tore a piece of bark from an old willow and gave it to Edgar. "I can brew this to make a tea to help my old achy rheumatism," he said.

"What's rheumatism?" asked Michelle.

"Well, old-timers like me have stiff joints . . ." Cornelius started to explain, when Russell suddenly grabbed Edgar's hat and tossed it to Abigail.

"Give it back," shouted Edgar.

"Furlings," said Cornelius. "We shall go home right now if you are not going to take this lesson seriously."

The Furlings promised to behave, but it didn't last long. Russell couldn't wait to see the big surprise, so he dashed off down the trail.

"Stop!" shouted Cornelius.

But Russell had run too far to hear

an empty bottle out the window, and it shattered on the road.

Russell opened one eye, then the other, and struggled to get up.

"You must be careful," Cornelius scolded him. "The world is a dangerous place."

The Furlings pumped Cornelius with questions about the car and the road. But, for once, Cornelius did not have ready answers.

"Not now," he said as he herded everyone off the road and back to the woods. "I want you to get away from this wretched place as quickly as possible."

So the Furlings marched on down the trail.

"How much longer before we see the big surprise?" asked Russell.

"I think we're here," said Cornelius.

Cornelius's warning. In fact, he had run right out of the forest and onto a road. Russell looked at the blacktop and tried to figure out what it was. He'd never seen a road before.

Suddenly a car sped around the curve. It was aimed right at Russell.

Terrified, Russell fell to the ground, curled up into a ball, and put his hands over his head.

Cornelius and the Furlings ran out of the forest just in time to see the car drive right over Russell. Edgar gasped!

The driver, who never saw Russell, threw

He parted some tall grass, and there at the edge of a stream was a small boat.

The Furlings were so excited they all piled in at once. Both Abigail and Russell grabbed the tiller.

"I get to steer," said Russell.

"Don't be silly," said Abigail. "You'll sink us."

"Will not," said Russell. "Give me a chance."

"You two settle down," said Cornelius as he stepped into the boat. "We will all get a chance."

"You row first," he told Abigail and Russell. But since they didn't know how, they splashed everyone with the oars.

"Stop, stop, stop!" Cornelius shouted. "Now, let's start over. Pull together. Stroke, stroke. Ah, that's so much better," he said as they eased out into the middle of the stream.

Meanwhile, back on the dreaded road, a big tanker truck was barrelling along—until it ran over the broken bottle and blew out a front tire.

The truck crashed into the guardrail, careened off the road, and landed on its side against a tree.

The driver could barely open the door as he staggered out. He saw a crack in the tank and smelled something foul. "The

chemicals are escaping," he gasped. "They're poisonous! I've got to get help."

At the same time, the Furlings' boating lessons were not going well. Abigail lost her paddle, so she grabbed Russell's.

Russell screamed, "You're going to lose my paddle, too!"

"I don't like this," said Edgar.

Cornelius started to say something, but Abigail and Russell stood up and the boat tipped over. Everyone fell into the water.

"Swim for shore," shouted Cornelius.

Safely on shore, they shook themselves dry, but Cornelius looked concerned and said, "Something's wrong. The woods are far too still. Even the birds have gone. We must hurry home."

Cornelius and the Furlings stopped in shock when they reached the crest of a hill where they could look down at their meadow. All the flowers and plants were

dead or wilting, the
leaves were falling off
the trees, the grass had
turned brown, and there wasn't a creature
in sight.

"Oh, dear heavens . . . not here," said
Cornelius.

Edgar said, "What's happened? Where is
everyone?"

Michelle called, "Mommy! Daddy!" and
ran toward her burrow.

"Stop," shouted Cornelius. "It's not safe."

Abigail, Russell, and Edgar raced off to
try to catch Michelle.

Michelle stopped at the entrance to her
burrow and called, "Mommy, are you
there?"

No one answered, so she rushed inside.

The other Furlings tried to follow her,
but Cornelius stopped them.

"You cannot go any farther," he said.
"I think some kind of poison has seeped
down into her burrow."

"What about Michelle?" said Edgar.

"Just a minute and I'll think of how we
might best proceed," said Cornelius.

"Well, I'm not waiting," said Abigail,
and she rushed inside to rescue Michelle.

"Cover your mouth and nose!" Cornelius
shouted after Abigail.

Abigail pulled the end of her shirt up
over her mouth and nose to protect herself
from the poisonous fumes as she descended
into Michelle's burrow.

The first thing she saw was Michelle's
parents lying by their dining table—dead!

Abigail was horrified.

She called for Michelle and heard a weak cough.

Michelle was sprawled on the floor on the other side of the table. Abigail touched her cheek, and Michelle coughed once again.

"Oh, Michelle, I am so glad you are still alive," whispered Abigail.

She began to pull Michelle up the stairs and out of her burrow, where Cornelius and the Furlings were anxiously waiting. Cornelius immediately bent to pick

Michelle up in his arms.

"Abigail," he said. "For once I am glad you did not listen to me. Hurry, Furlings, we must get her to my house. It's on higher ground, and we should be safe there."

"But what about *our* parents?" Abigail, Edgar, and Russell all asked at once.

"I fear for the worst," said Cornelius.

As the sad group of Furlings headed back to Cornelius's house, the flower fell out of Michelle's hair and wilted.

"Are we the only ones left?" asked Abigail.

Edgar cried, "I was in such a hurry this morning, I didn't kiss Mama goodbye."

Russell asked, "How did the poison get into our homes, Cornelius?"

"HUMANS," said Cornelius. "They've always been a threat to us. When I was a Furling, humans wedged a trap into

the entrance of our burrow. My father saw that there was room for me and my sister to slip through, so we ran and hid in a hollow log until the humans went away.

"There was nothing we could do to rescue my mother and father, but there is something we can do to save Michelle."

"What can we do?" said Edgar.

"We need to find special herbs for medicine," said Cornelius, consulting one of his big books. "Eyebright to soothe the burns on her eyes, and lungwort for her damaged lungs."

"But the poison has killed everything in our meadow," said Abigail.

"Then you must find another meadow," said Cornelius, "and you only have two days' time. We must have these herbs before the moon waxes full, or it will be too late to save Michelle."

"You'll show us how to find the herbs, right?" asked Russell.

"I wish I could," said Cornelius. "But I can't leave poor Michelle alone. You'll need an early start, so get a good night's rest."

At dawn the next morning the Furlings tiptoed over to Michelle's bed. She

was barely breathing. Edgar gently tucked in her covers.

"We must get ready," said Abigail. "Our time is very short."

Russell collected an armful of nuts and berries, and he picked up a paper from Cornelius's workbench to bundle the food into his pack.

"This isn't a picnic," said Abigail. "Pack something useful." She tossed Russell a rope.

Abigail rolled up a ball of string and put it in her pocket.

Edgar took a magnifying glass.

"You must take my map," said Cornelius. "It will guide you to the edge of

Dapplewood Forest. Then you must seek another meadow on your own."

The Furlings walked and walked, over hills, through bramble bushes, and over slippery rocks to cross a stream. It began to grow dark, and Russell started to lag behind the others.

"Wait," said Edgar. "Haven't we come far enough for one day?"

"We have to keep going," said Abigail.

"Look, the moon is out. Cornelius said we have to get those plants back to Michelle before it turns full!"

"There's a clearing ahead, but is it safe to cross?" asked Edgar. "There's no cover."

"You're right," said Abigail. "But let's run for that dead tree and then plan our next move."

What the Furlings did not know was that the one-eyed owl was watching them from its nest in the old tree.

Russell collapsed and said, "I can't run any farther with this pack on my back."

"Give it to me," said Abigail. "We can't stop here."

"I'm a little worried about this place," said Edgar.

Just as Russell was handing over his pack, the owl darted out of the tree, swooped across the clearing, and grabbed Abigail.

Russell, still holding on to one side of his pack, was yanked upward with Abigail by the owl.

Edgar quickly snatched Russell's tail to pull them back down, but the owl carried him away as well.

The Furlings screamed. Abigail had to let go of the pack, and Russell and Edgar crashed back to the ground.

"Help!" cried Abigail as the owl carried her towards its nest.

"Take that!" Abigail shouted as she grabbed a thorn from the side of the nest and stabbed the owl's leg.

The owl shrieked and dropped Abigail in his nest, where she quickly hid under some twigs. Meanwhile Russell had started up the tree to help Abigail.

"We're going to climb?" asked Edgar.

"We can't dig our way up," answered Russell.

The owl furiously searched his nest for Abigail. Remembering the magnifying glass that she had taken from Edgar, Abigail held it up in front of her mouth and bared her teeth. She must have looked like a wild beast when he finally saw her.

The startled owl jumped backward and knocked Abigail out of the nest with his wing. She fell through the air and landed right on top of Edgar and Russell.

"Let's get out of here," said Russell.

"That was too close!" said Edgar.

Abigail said, "Thanks for coming to my rescue."

"Glad to help," said Edgar.

The three tired Furlings huddled together by the side of a log to sleep through the rest of the night.

The next morning the Furlings were awakened by a group of birds, who were moaning and crying as they marched beside the spot where the Furlings had been sleeping.

One named Phineas said, "Yellow Dragons have drained our nesting ground and turned it into a muddy graveyard. Now our poor Bosworth is gone forever."

"If that's Bosworth, he doesn't look dead to me," said Abigail. "He's just stuck up to his knees in the mud."

Edgar turned to Phineas and said, "We can save Bosworth."

"That would take a miracle," said Phineas.

But the Furlings had an idea. They took their rope and a big stick and popped Bosworth right out of the mud. Bosworth flew up into the air and landed in his mother's arms.

"Hallelujah! I hope you plan on staying to help us celebrate," Phineas shouted to the Furlings.

"I'm sorry, but we can't," said Abigail. "We have to find a new meadow before nightfall."

Phineas said, "There's a glorious meadow called Oakdale just yonder, but you have to get past the Yellow Dragons to reach it."

"Are the Yellow Dragons terrible?" asked Edgar.

"They are huge monsters that breathe fire and smoke," said Phineas.

Edgar gasped, and Abigail said, "Don't

worry, we can take care of ourselves."

"After what you did for Bosworth, I truly believe you can," said Phineas as he pointed the way toward the meadow.

The Furlings walked in that direction and found themselves in a barren, dreary place, full of nothing but freshly dug holes, piles of dirt, and shattered rocks.

"Did the Yellow Dragons do this?" asked Russell.

Before anyone could answer, the Furlings were engulfed in clouds of dust. Coughing and sneezing, they looked up and saw the giant jaws of a steam shovel hovering over their heads.

They screamed and ran. A yellow bulldozer rumbled towards them. Russell dropped to the ground and curled up into a ball, as hedgehogs do. Edgar and Abigail rolled him over to some sewer pipes, where they hid.

Then another Yellow Dragon came along and scooped up the sewer pipes. The Furlings tumbled over one another until they fell out the end of the pipe.

A large backhoe took a big bite of earth right next to the Furlings.

"I think it wants to eat us," said Abigail.

"Not that one, but maybe this one does," said Edgar, as another giant bulldozer roared towards the Furlings.

They scrambled out of its way but ran right into the path of a huge steamroller.

The Furlings screamed and dived into a ditch, where they landed on top of a drain grate. Edgar and Abigail grabbed onto the bars as they slipped through the grating, but Russell got stuck.

"Suck in your stomach. You've got to slide through!" shouted Edgar.

"Russell! Wriggle hard," said Abigail. "It's coming fast!"

It was no use. Russell was stuck. Edgar and Abigail let go of the grate and each grabbed one of Russell's feet. They swung and pulled as hard as they could until Russell finally squeezed through just as the steamroller smashed over the drain grate. The three Furlings tumbled all the way down to the bottom of a sewer.

"Help! Help! I'm drowning," shouted Edgar.

Abigail laughed and said, "Stand up, Edgar."

Edgar laughed, too, as he stood up and saw that the water barely covered his feet. He wiped his glasses clean and looked down the sewer's long tunnel.

"Wow! Look at this place!" said Russell.

"It gives me the creeps," Edgar shuddered.

Abigail said, "We're only underground."

"Yeah, and you're a mole—right?" said Russell. "Think of this as home—only stinky."

"That's not very funny," said Edgar.

"We're not helping Michelle by just standing around," said Abigail. "We've got to get moving."

Just then the Furlings heard a loud rumbling noise.

Abigail shouted, "Look out!" as a wall of water rushed over them.

The dirty water was filled with dead leaves and all kinds of debris. It swept the little Furlings right off their feet.

"What's happening?" sputtered Russell.

"Keep your head up!" shouted Abigail.

The Furlings struggled to stay afloat as the rushing water hurled them through the

"This lake is not on the map."

"It's all over," sighed Abigail. "We'll never find our way now."

"Don't say that, Abigail. Michelle's counting on us," said Russell.

"Poor Cornelius must be worried about us," said Abigail.

"Maybe if we climb that hill," Edgar suggested, "we can see where we are."

When the Furlings reached the top of the hill, Russell said, "Boy, we could be any place." But just then a darting butterfly caught his eye as it flew across a faint trail. "Look!" he shouted, "There's a path leading down to a meadow."

"It must be Oakdale," said Edgar.

"We made it!" cheered the Furlings as they ran down the path.

long and twisting sewer pipe. Then, just when they could not keep their heads above water a moment longer, the Furlings burst through an opening and were dumped into a lake.

Gasping and moaning, the bedraggled Furlings swam to shore.

When he had caught his breath, Edgar stood up, took the map out of his pocket, and wrung the water out of it.

As he spread it open, Russell asked, "Now where are we?"

"I don't know," answered Edgar.

"Now all we need to do is collect the eyebright and . . ." Edgar was saying when suddenly he was bumped off his feet by a gopher. The gopher, George, and another Oakdale creature, Willy the Woodmouse, were fighting over an acorn.

"Are you all right, Edgar?" asked Abigail.

Before Edgar could say a word, Waggs the Squirrel ran in, jumped over the Furlings, and followed Willy and the acorn up a tree. Then a gang of other mice and squirrels dashed up after Waggs and Willy.

"Gee, I thought meals were out of control at my house," said Russell.

Edgar asked, "How are we going to get anybody to help us find the herbs?"

"Maybe these guys won't be so grouchy after they eat," said Russell.

"Well, we can't wait that long," said Abigail. And she climbed up the tree and grabbed Willy by the ankle.

"Hey! Let go!" cried Willy.

Abigail hung on tight, and they both lost their balance and fell to the ground.

The acorn was knocked out of Willy's hand. George the Gopher ran up, grabbed it, and dashed back underground.

Willy started to yell at Abigail, but then he realized he had never before seen such a beautiful little woodmouse. "Gosh, I hope I didn't hurt you," he said.

"No, I'm fine," sighed Abigail as she realized she had never before seen such a handsome woodmouse.

"Wow, look at all the eyebright!" yelled Russell. "The lungwort can't be too far away."

"Too far for the likes of you," sneered Waggs as he pointed to a clump of lungwort high up on the side of a rocky cliff, out of reach.

from a tree and sewed them together with a giant pine needle.

They found wood for a mast and used string to stitch the leaves to the mast.

"I think this might really work," said Edgar.

"To your stations . . ." said Russell.

Russell sat behind the steering wheel, and Abigail and Edgar got ready to crank the winder-upper.

They cranked, and the wings started to flap up and down. The Wingamathing lifted off the ground and skimmed over the lake.

"Yea! We're flying," shouted Russell.

"They did it," hollered Willy.

Waggs and all the other Oakdale animals looked up at the Furlings in amazement.

Russell shouted, "I'm going to glide by the cliff, Abigail. Climb out on the wing and get ready to grab the lungwort."

"Don't worry," said Russell. "We've already got a plan."

Edgar looked at Abigail, who had not taken her eyes off Willy, and said, "Are we still in this together or not?"

"Of course we are," said Abigail. "What's your plan, Russell?"

Because Russell always thought better on a full stomach, he sat down and opened his pack to get something to eat. Munching away, he nearly spit out his food when he saw it had been wrapped up in Cornelius's plans for the Wingamathing. When he held up the diagram, Edgar said, "Whoopee, we will *fly* to the top of that cliff!"

Waggs doubled over in laughter.

"Laugh all you want. We'll show you," said Abigail.

And the Furlings got to work following Cornelius's plan. They gathered leaves

Suddenly the wind blew Edgar's scarf into Russell's face, blinding him temporarily.

The wind wrapped the scarf around Russell's head. As he struggled to get it off, the Wingamathing bumped against the side of the cliff, plunging Abigail towards the ground.

Willy was horrified as he watched from the meadow.

When Russell freed himself of the scarf, he immediately put the Wingamathing into a steep dive to catch Abigail.

As they swooped beneath her, Edgar grabbed Abigail and swung her safely into the cockpit.

"We'll have to try again," said Russell.

"It's no use," said Abigail. "The wing scraped all the lungwort off the cliff."

"Don't worry. I've got it," shouted Edgar as he scooped the lungwort off the tip of the wing.

Willy and all the rest of the animals cheered, "They got it!"

Russell turned the Wingamathing around to fly home.

"Look, the land of the Yellow Dragons," said Abigail. They flew high above the steam shovel, the backhoe, the bulldozers, and the steamroller.

Edgar rolled out the map and sketched in all the new places the Furlings had discovered—including Oakdale—and said, "Won't Cornelius be excited to see where we have been!"

"Hey, I can't see much at all," said Abigail.

The sky had suddenly grown dark. It was filled with storm clouds. Lightning began to flash around the Furlings' airship.

Edgar quickly rolled up the map and

stuffed it down into his shirt.

Russell could hardly steer through the wind and heavy rain. They dived down by the trees and nearly crashed into a barn.

Russel shouted to Abigail and Edgar, "Crank as hard as you can, we have to get up higher!"

Abigail and Edgar cranked the winder-upper as fast as they could to get the wings flapping up and down again. At the same time, Russell struggled to pull back the wheel and to bring the plane up out of its treacherous dive. It worked.

But the Furlings were not safe for long. The wind then blew them into the wires of a utility pole, causing an explosion that set their wing on fire. Plummeting towards earth, the Wingamathing crash-landed, skidded across a field, and finally came to a stop against an old willow tree.

Though dazed, Edgar examined the tree and took a piece of bark out of his pocket.

"Look! The 'rheumatism' tree from our hike," he said.

"We're home!" the Furlings all shouted at the same time.

"Come on! Let's get to Michelle," said Abigail.

The Furlings ran to Cornelius's house, where they saw a light in the window.

"Are we in time?" asked Russell.

"I'm afraid she's slipping away. We must administer the herbs immediately," said Cornelius.

A sudden, loud clanking noise startled the Furlings.

"Come here quick!" called Edgar, as he looked out the window.

"Oh, no . . . not again," said Cornelius. "It's the HUMANS."

Abigail and Russell dashed over to the window to see what was happening.

The humans tromped through the forest, wearing heavy boots and bulky suits. They had masks over their heads and wore special breathing gear to protect them

from any remaining toxic fumes.

Cornelius picked up Michelle, and they escaped out the back door—which, given his parents' fate, Cornelius had been careful to provide in his own burrow.

Edgar had never used this door before, and in the dark he tripped, fell, and lost his glasses. Before anyone could help him, Edgar stumbled into an old box trap, and the door slammed shut behind him.

Edgar scrambled back and forth inside the box trap and cried out.

One of the humans heard him, knelt down beside the trap, and shined his light on Edgar.

Covering his eyes, Edgar squashed himself as far back in the trap as he could. But the human reached inside and lifted Edgar out.

Cornelius and the other Furlings had watched everything from their hiding place and were worried sick about Edgar.

The human looked carefully at Edgar and then set him down on the ground, pushed him a little, and said, "There you go, little fellow."

Edgar raced over to Cornelius and the other Furlings in their hiding place.

Then the human unexpectedly crushed the old box trap with his foot, picked it up, and carried it away.

"In all my days, I've never seen anything like that," said Cornelius.

Abigail found Edgar's glasses, carefully wiped them clean, and handed them back to her friend.

Cornelius patted Edgar on the head and said, "Thank goodness!"

With Cornelius carrying Michelle, the three Furlings led the way back to the old willow tree.

"We'll be safe here," said Abigail.

Russell took the precious herbs out of his pack and handed them to Cornelius.

Edgar cradled Michelle's head while Cornelius squeezed liquid from the lungwort into her mouth.

Then Cornelius gently put some of the eyebright on Michelle's eyelids.

Michelle coughed weakly.

"Did we make it in time?" Edgar asked Cornelius.

"We won't know until the morning," Cornelius said. "But whatever happens, you've done all that you could for Michelle."

The Furlings snuggled together on the ground beside Cornelius and eventually fell asleep.

The next morning, Russell reached out his hand to touch Michelle, but she did not respond.

"Poor Michelle," said Edgar.

"We were too late," said Abigail.

Cornelius began to sob. One of his tears dropped onto Michelle's nose, and she moved.

Michelle slowly opened her eyes.

"Thank goodness!" exclaimed Cornelius. "You're all right!"

"I . . . I think so . . . " said Michelle.

The Furlings jumped up and down with

joy and crowded up close to hug Michelle.

"Great Honk!" shouted Cornelius as he looked past the Furlings. "My Flapper Wingamathing!"

"We built it," said Edgar.

"And we flew it," added Russell.

"Magnificent!" exclaimed Cornelius.

"Look, Uncle Cornelius," squeaked Michelle as Russell's family, Abigail's dad, and Edgar's mother poked their heads out of the thicket.

Edgar rushed up to kiss his Mama.

"Uncle Cornelius," said Michelle, "all the mommies and daddies are coming back."

"Not all of them," Cornelius said sadly as

he picked Michelle up in his arms. "I know
I'll never be able to replace your own
mommy and daddy, but I'll do my best to
take care of you."

Michelle sniffled, now remembering the
horrible sight of her parents lying
dead, and she finally said, "I guess nothing
will ever be the same again, will it,
Uncle Cornelius?"

Cornelius thought a moment and said,
"Not exactly the same, Michelle, but if
we all work as hard to save Dapplewood
as your three friends worked to save
you, it will be beautiful in time."

Published by Turner Publishing, Inc.

A Subsidiary of Turner Broadcasting System, Inc.

One CNN Center, Box 105366

Atlanta, Georgia 30348-5366

First Edition 10 9 8 7 6 5 4 3 2

Once Upon a Forest

Adaptation by Elizabeth Isele

Based upon characters created by Rae Lambert and
a screenplay written by Mark Young and Kelly Ward

Illustrated by Carol H. Grosvenor

ISBN 1-878685-87-2

Distributed by Andrews and McMeel

A Universal Press Syndicate Company

4900 Main Street

Kansas City, Missouri 64112

Editorial

Walton Rawls, *Vice President Editorial*

Katherine Buttler, *Associate Editor*

Crawford Barnett, *Copy Editor*

Design

Michael J. Walsh, *Vice President Design/Production*

Elaine Streithof, *Book Design*

The illustrator wishes to acknowledge the following people for their help:

Charles Grosvenor, Donna Prince, and Tim Barnes.

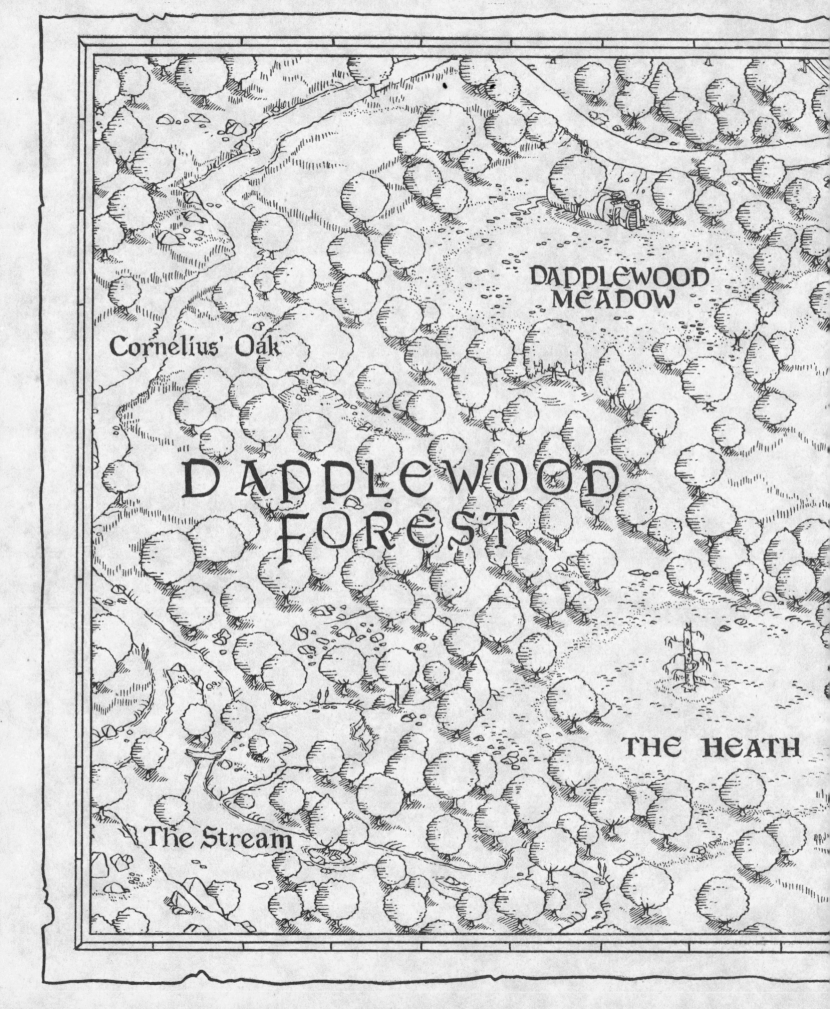

DAPPLEWOOD
MEADOW

Cornelius' Oak

DAPPLEWOOD
FOREST

THE HEATH

The Stream